The Frog Castle

Also by Jostein Gaarder

STORIES FOR YOUNGER CHILDREN

Hello? Is Anybody There?
The Christmas Mystery

FICTION FOR OLDER READERS

Through a Glass Darkly
The Solitaire Mystery
Sophie's World

Jostein Gaarder

The Frog Castle

Translated by James Anderson
Illustrated by Philip Hopman

Orion
Children's Books

First published in Great Britain in 1999
by Orion Children's Books
a division of the Orion Publishing Group Ltd
Orion House
5 Upper St Martin's Lane
London WC2H 9EA

Originally published in Norwegian under the title *Froskeslottet* in 1994
© 1994 by H. Aschehoug & Co. (W. Nygaard), Oslo
English Translation © James Anderson 1999
Illustrations © Philip Hopman 1999

A catalogue record for this book is
available from the British Library.

Typeset at The Spartan Press Ltd,
Lymington, Hants

Printed and bound in Great Britain by
Butler & Tanner Ltd, Frome and London

Contents

The Frog Castle

1

The Moonlight

I'm not really quite sure how it began, but I remember walking out into the moonlight across the frozen snow. That was quite strange for a start; children don't usually take forest walks alone at night, with the moon floating like a fat balloon over the spruce trees. But it wasn't the only strange thing about this particular night.

Just as I'd passed the big pond where Dad and I used to lie on our stomachs searching for tadpoles, I suddenly caught sight of a boggart. This wouldn't have been so odd if he'd come stealing out from amongst the trees, for example, but that wasn't the way he made his entrance.

I was sitting on the snow puzzling about something I'd forgotten. All of a sudden, the boggart appeared out of thin air, as if he'd slipped out of somewhere else and into the forest where I was sitting. Apart from the red boggart cap, which all boggarts have, his clothes were green. He was a bit smaller than me – though he was well and truly grown-up.

'Well, well,' he said at last when he was as plain as the trees around us. As he spoke, he pulled one of his arms out of the other side of thin air.

'Well, well,' he repeated emphatically.

What a funny way to start a conversation, I thought. Saying 'well, well' means that all you've got to say is that you want the other person to speak.

'Well, well, what?' I asked timidly.

He looked up at me, narrowing his eyes as if he wasn't quite at home in the moonlight.

'So, you're taking a stroll,' he said.

But that wasn't much of a comment either. We could both see that I was taking a stroll, because we were standing in the snow by the Newt Pond.

I felt like saying no just to trick him. Instead I said: 'It looks like we both are.'

I thought it a perfectly good answer, but he didn't.

'*I'm* not parading about in the moonlight wearing nothing but my nightclothes,' he said.

At that I gazed down at my pale blue pyjamas, which were covered with pictures of cars and motorbikes. I hadn't realised they were all I was wearing, and I felt like creeping away to hide. But it's not so easy to hide from a boggart who's just caught you red-handed.

'They're very comfortable in all weathers,' I said in as grown-up a tone as I could manage. 'And if you think wearing nightclothes is strange, I think being a boggart is even stranger.'

But he was pointing up at me again. He had obviously made up his mind to win this tussle.

'The funniest thing of all is that you're walking barefoot in the snow. You must be very poor indeed if you can't afford a pair of slippers.'

I was forced to look down at my legs again, and now I was even more embarrassed than I'd been over my pyjamas. I discovered my feet were completely naked, and also that my toes felt very cold. How nice a warm duvet would be, I thought, but it was such a stupid idea I didn't dare mention it. You can't go dragging a duvet about in the middle of the forest, even if there's a full moon and the snow is frozen.

'My mum and dad are very rich,' I retorted. 'For a start, we've got a big house with a terrace and deck chairs. If they wanted to, they could buy thousands of pairs of slippers, but they say it's healthy to walk about without shoes on, and sometimes they call me a little prince.'

This last piece of information made an impression on him.

'And what might the prince's name be?' he asked after making a deep bow.

'My name is Gregory Peggory,' I replied with dignity. This wasn't strictly true, but I could hardly say my name was Gregory Green, or he'd never

believe I was a real prince.

'Most interesting,' he observed. 'You see, I've read in an old book that princes like you are extremely fond of pancakes and strawberry jam, and it just so happens I've made a whole load of pancakes. As for strawberries, well, I've got more than enough of those in the garden.'

I didn't believe a word of it. When grown-ups want to create an impression, they always boast about things like making pancakes. I looked down at the snow, thinking it wasn't the right time of year for strawberries. But I didn't dare contradict him, because I knew that boggarts are much wiser than children.

If it hadn't been for his red boggart cap and all

the wrinkles on his face, I'd have taken him for a child. Now I noticed that he was a teeny bit melancholy too, though his eyes were as blue as two huge blueberries.

'Would you like to try them?' he asked.

'Your blueberries?' I said in alarm.

At that he just stood there shaking his head.

'I invite a lone nocturnal wanderer to freshly made pancakes and strawberry jam,' he said. 'I do this, even though he's tripping about in the cold snow without any shoes. And how does this little Peggory prince repay me? He starts asking for blueberries instead. It's that sort of thing that's turned us forest boggarts into a very unhappy race. You said it yourself just a moment ago. I'm a teeny bit melancholy, you said.'

I had to think back hard about whether I'd said anything of the sort, I only recalled thinking it, and that's not quite the same thing.

'We're debating a very simple problem, really,' the boggart went on. 'Do you want to eat pancakes and strawberry jam from my own garden, or would you rather wander about in semi-darkness? Because pancakes and strawberry jam are what's on the menu.'

It was exactly like listening to Dad. He was always asking what was on the menu. I'd always imagined that the menu was another word for stove, because that was where the food was, but no stove was visible out there in the moonlight.

'But you haven't got a stove,' I said.

He stood there dumbfounded. Then he began to dig inside his ears with his fingers.

'I beg your pardon, Prince Peggory, there must be something in my ears, because I didn't quite catch what you said.'

'You haven't got a stove,' I repeated.

'You don't go lugging a great stove around each time you go out to take a peep at the moon,' he said.

Now it was my turn to reach for my ears, I had to see whether they were still there or had dropped off. Luckily they were as firmly in place as my nose.

My feet were getting colder and colder.

'There's a bit of a draught here, I'm afraid,' said the boggart. 'It's hardly surprising. The whole forest is wide open.'

When he said wide open, it made me think of fierce animal jaws and I felt a bit scared in case a wolf or a lion should suddenly appear. I began to feel worried about what we might end up discussing if we stood there talking any more. So I said:

'I'd really like some pancakes and strawberry jam, if they're still on the menu.'

At that he gave a grin and licked his lips a couple of times, once on each side of his mouth.

'That was a mature decision,' he said, 'and particularly apt as I've a houseful of ripe wild strawberries.'

Neither his house nor the strawberries could be seen. All I could make out was the moonlight on the trees and the crusted snow.

'Where is the house with the strawberries?' I asked warily.

'It's in the middle of summer,' he said. 'And that's just round the corner. But you can't go there in just your nightclothes.'

He'd hardly finished speaking when I suddenly found myself clad in different clothes. I was wearing green silk trousers and a silk shirt that was as red as a strawberry.

I was absolutely astounded at this, but pretended not to notice.

'You must take my hand, Gregory Peggory,' he said.

I realised I didn't know his name, and Mum had told me I wasn't to let strange people take me to their homes. I was sure this applied to strange boggarts as well.

'What's your name?' I asked.

He flourished one arm and bowed very gallantly. 'I'm just called Umpin.'

He took my hand, and we walked straight out of the winter scene. When we came out on the other side, it was a hot summer's day. We were in exactly the same spot holding hands by the Newt Pond. But now the sun was shining.

2

Pancakes

'What shall we do first?' asked Umpin the boggart. 'Shall we catch newts first and then have pancakes and strawberry jam, or eat pancakes and strawberry jam first and then catch tadpoles?'

I didn't think that was enough choice: I wanted to have pancakes first and then catch newts afterwards.

'We must eat up the pancakes before someone comes along and takes them off the menu,' I said.

He looked up at me, perplexed.

'I won't have any niggling,' he said. 'It's the only thing we boggarts can't bear. We generally bend over backwards for real Peggory princes, but my great-grandfather once bent over backwards so far that he went snap.'

I stared down at him without saying a word.

'Be careful now,' he said, 'on one occasion my great-grandmother was so surprised at hearing some strange words that her eyes popped out. For years and years they rolled about all over the forest. That's why there are so many blueberries here, and why boggarts don't have pancakes with blueberry jam. But that's enough, now we must be getting a move on. My little house is in this direction.'

We began making our way into the forest. Soon we arrived at the stoutest tree I'd ever seen. Though very broad, it was a lot shorter than the surrounding trees. By and by I realised that it was just a trunk or a root. All around the thick bole grew millions of wild strawberries.

I assumed this was Umpin's house and that all the wild strawberries were his garden, but I wasn't completely sure until he opened a door in the tree-trunk.

'Welcome to my house, Gregory Peggory!' Umpin said grandly.

We went in, and I found myself in the smallest house I'd seen since the last time I'd got inside my cousin Flora's dolls' house. Flora lived way down south. It looked so like her dolls' house that at first I was a bit worried in case the boggart had been to Flora's during the night and stolen all her dolls' things while she was asleep. But Flora's house was miles away and it took hours to drive there, and I didn't think boggarts drove cars. So it was obviously just that it bore a strong resemblance.

At that moment I noticed a huge stack of pancakes. It wasn't on the menu, but on a tiny little table, next to a big jamjar.

We each sat down on a green chair and helped ourselves to a pancake. There had been so much talk of wild strawberries, that I had to ask Umpin if the jam could turn wild, too. This was clearly a mistake, for the boggart looked upset again.

'I'm only used to eating ordinary strawberries,' I had to explain, 'and they can be pretty difficult at times too . . .'

He shook his head.

'Gregory Peggory,' he said, 'I've reached a solemn agreement with all my wild strawberries that they should behave in my garden. In return, I've given them permission to play havoc with any young prince who doesn't want to eat my jam.'

At this I hastily spread a load of jam on my pancake, because the wild strawberries looked as if they might be misbehaving already.

'How good were they?' he asked after we'd eaten four or five pancakes each.

'Very good,' I replied.

But the boggart wasn't content with my
answer.

'I don't think you listened properly to my
question,' he observed. 'I said *how* good. If
someone asks how old you are, it's no good saying
very old.'

But I didn't know how to explain how good the

pancakes were.

'Five and a half,' I guessed.

Umpin began to clear the table.

'That's the very last time,' he said flatly. 'Not long ago I was visited by another Peggory prince, and he said I was a man of a thousand talents.'

Just then I had a bright idea.

'What I meant was five and a half thousand, of course.'

Umpin began to dance around the table, and finally he jumped up and gave me a little kiss on the cheek.

'Now we can go out into the summer sunshine and catch tadpoles,' he said.

He snatched up an empty jamjar from the sideboard.

3

Tadpoles

I'd been to the big Newt Pond in the forest many times before, but today everything seemed different. The trees were even greener than usual and the sky was as blue as paint. And the twigs didn't hurt my feet even though I was walking barefoot.

The boggart lay down on his stomach by the water's edge and searched for tadpoles.

'Did you know that tadpoles can turn into frogs?' he asked with his head almost in the water.

But I didn't bother to answer, because everyone knows that. Instead I said:

'We'll have to catch hundreds of tadpoles to make enough for a whole frog.'

Umpin held up his jamjar and showed me the three he'd caught already.

'But perhaps you didn't know that frogs turn into princes when you kiss them, and that princes have huge castles where lots of exciting things are always happening.'

I knew that too. Grandad had once told me about a frog who'd turned into a prince just because some spoilt girl had kissed him smack on his shiny mouth. But if I'd said I knew that as well, the boggart would certainly be put out because he wasn't cleverer than me. And if I said I *didn't* know, then he'd think me terribly stupid.

Luckily I didn't have to answer, because at that moment Umpin raised his jar from the water. It was brimful of tadpoles.

'We must stir the contents with a magic stick,' he said.

I walked up the path and found a stick, but I had no idea if it was a magic stick or not. You can never tell that before you've used it.

It was a magic stick. Umpin only had to dip it into the jar once and all the little tadpoles turned into one big frog.

'Beautiful!' he said, waving the magic stick in the air.

I'd never thought frogs looked particularly

beautiful, I liked little tadpoles much better.

Just then the frog jumped out of the jar, landed on a stone and sat peering up at us. Its heart was throbbing so hard that the poor frog bobbed up and down, up and down. Next to it was the jamjar with nothing but water in it. Not a single tadpole was left.

'But we're only half way there,' Umpin muttered.

I didn't understand what he meant.

'Which of us shall kiss it?' he went on.

'Not me at any rate,' I said quickly. I didn't want to kiss the horrible frog.

'We *must* kiss it if it's to turn into a prince,' said Umpin. 'And I think it's strange that you can't do it.'

'Why?' I asked, feeling as if I was going to cry.

'Because you were once a frog yourself,' Umpin said, pointing up at me with the magic stick.

At that I really did begin to cry.

'I've never . . . been a frog,' I managed to sob at last.

Instead of comforting me the boggart merely shook his head.

'Gregory Peggory,' he began. 'Didn't we agree that you're a real prince? Or did I let you eat my pancakes under false pretences?'

I could only stand and stare open-mouthed.

'And didn't we also agree about where princes come from?' Umpin went on impatiently.

His question struck me like a bolt of lightning.

'So, then, aren't we agreed that you were once a frog?'

He peered up at me with his blueberry eyes. Just then I couldn't have cared if they had fallen out.

'I come from my mum's tummy,' I said. 'And I got there because Dad kissed her. And then some small things swam out of Dad and into her tummy.'

Even to my ears this explanation seemed so long and complicated that it sounded like some excuse. Perhaps that was why Umpin seated himself on a tree stump and mopped his brow as if he were exhausted. The frog only puffed itself up on the nearby stone.

'Let's take things one at a time,' said the boggart. 'Just *what* were these small things that swam into your mum's tummy? They couldn't have been tadpoles, by any chance? You said he kissed her,

too. Is that any better than kissing a frog? And then again, hasn't your mum or dad ever called you a little toad? And how do you think you managed to survive inside a tummy if you couldn't swim like a frog?'

I couldn't think of anything to say in reply, but I felt I hated both the frog and the boggart.

Once more Umpin pointed up at me with his magic stick.

'Hate the frog if you want,' he said. 'I only ask that you give it a little peck on the mouth. Because if you don't, we'll never get to the great castle, and then there won't be any fairy tale, either.'

I could see I had no choice. The boggart would tap me with his magic stick and turn me into a frog again if I wasn't obedient. If a frog really could turn into a prince, then a prince could surely turn into a frog as well.

I crouched down on the ground and kissed the slimy frog so hard that my lips got all covered in frog-spittle.

4

Prince Garamond

'Greetings!' said the prince.

The frog had vanished the instant I'd kissed it and, in its place, a real prince stood before us. He wore a long blue velvet cloak, on his head was a small gold crown studded with rubies, and from the silver belt round his waist hung a proper sword.

I felt rather stupid standing between him and Umpin. I was no more than a common forest prince, while he was a genuine royal prince, I could see that straight away.

'And your name, prince?' Umpin asked.

'My name is Garamond,' the other answered with
a dignified look. 'But that was a very long time
ago.'

I didn't know what he meant. Neither did
Umpin.

'I was once crown prince at the great castle over
there,' he explained. 'But then one day I had a spell

cast on me and got turned into a thousand tadpoles. It was because I wouldn't surrender my heart to a wicked boggart who lived in a tree-trunk just below the castle. But you two have made me whole again, and I'm grateful for your efforts.'

I turned and looked at Umpin. He was clearly not feeling so perky now. At least, there weren't any offers of pancakes with strawberry jam this time. But he did say:

'Most interesting. But that could never have been a boggart from my family. We're not that heartless.'

'Nonsense!' retorted the prince. 'No boggarts have live hearts like frogs or people. That's why they can only exist in people's imaginations. And why they're always on the look out for human hearts. And they hunt for them when the snow is frozen and the moon is full . . . '

Was it really possible that the pancakes and the strawberry jam had merely been bait, and that Umpin had actually wanted to steal my heart?

'I think we should talk about the castle instead,' said Umpin emphatically. 'If you're a real, royal prince you must live in

a great white castle
with lofty towers and
lots of servants.'

Garamond gave a
haughty nod, and just
then we glimpsed his
castle on a rise behind the
Newt Pond.

'Extraordinary!'
exclaimed the boggart,
scratching his head with his
chubby fingers. 'I've lived
here by this pond for more than
eleven years, and I've never noticed that beautiful
castle.'

Dad and I had come here lots of times, too, and
hadn't spotted so much as a turret.

Garamond adjusted his crown with its red rubies
and said:

'Surely you don't think you can bring a prince
who's been bewitched back to life and everything
will be exactly like it was before?'

With that he put two fingers to his lips and gave
a whistle so shrill that it could be heard all over the
forest. A moment later a great carriage appeared,
drawn by eight frogs. They just appeared from the
depths of the forest and drove up on to the path.

I'd never seen frogs like this before, but I'd
heard they could be found in South America. They
were smaller than horses, but they were every bit as
big as Alsatian dogs.

'Climb aboard, and welcome to my castle,' said
Garamond, opening the carriage door.

We got into the carriage, and the frogs began to

hop along the path with us in tow. It jolted and
rattled so much that I felt as if my heart was being
hurled about in my chest.

It reminded me of Grandad, who'd suddenly
got a pain in his heart and died. It had happened
only a few days after Mum had left for France.

5

The
Newts

'You must be on your best behaviour and watch
out for the newts,' said Garamond as we lurched
through the castle gates.

'The newts?' queried Umpin.

'They're the soldiers at the castle. And as I was
about to explain, they've never been particularly
keen either on boggarts or on Peggory princes. But
possibly they'll revise their opinion when they learn
that you've reassembled me.'

We were approaching the castle, and could now
see all the newt soldiers before the great entrance.
They were much bigger than the newts that lived in
the pond; they were the same size as Garamond,

and he was almost grown up. But they had tails just like the newts that Dad sometimes allowed to crawl up his arm. They all wore long swords. Because they were clothed in newt skin, they needed no armour.

When we got out of the carriage, four of the newts walked up to Garamond and greeted him by clashing their swords above his head.

'How has His Highness enjoyed himself in the pond?' one asked.

'It was most refreshing,' Garamond answered. 'But it's hard to keep track of yourself when there are so many of you.'

He waved courteously at Umpin and me.

'These two came to the rescue after they'd helped themselves from the menu. They put me together again, though their original plan was to catch newts.'

The soldiers drew themselves up, while Umpin and I did the exact opposite, we tried to make ourselves as small as possible.

'Prince Garamond!' continued the newt who'd been speaking. 'You can't have forgotten the queen forbade boggarts or Peggory princes to be brought into the castle?'

At that moment a whole lot of newts came swarming down the steps from the castle.

'The king's heart has been stolen!' they shouted. Immediately, Garamond began running up the steps, and as neither Umpin nor I had any desire to be left alone with the newts, we raced up after him.

We soon found ourselves in a large blue room. The king was lying on a bed of red silk. He didn't breathe or open his eyes. Garamond placed his sword on a round table and opened his arms wide.

'Don't leave me, Father!' he wailed.

The newts left the prince alone with his grief.

Umpin and I remained standing behind him, and we shed a few tears as well.

After a while a woman came in from the next room. She had a long blue skirt, and she wasn't wearing anything at all on top. I thought that a grown-up lady could at least put on a T-shirt when she had visitors.

Garamond threw his arms around her.

'Mother!' he whispered. 'Father is dead.'

When she caught sight of us, her eyes looked as if they were about to pop out of their sockets.

'Garamond!' she said. 'Isn't that the boggart who stole the king's heart?'

But Garamond didn't have time to answer.

'NEWTS!' shouted the queen, and four stout newts appeared at the door.

The queen pointed down at Umpin.

'So, you've admitted a boggart while I was grieving over the loss of my dear husband's heart?'

'Forgive us, honoured queen,' said one, 'but it wasn't our wish . . . '

'To the dungeon with him immediately!' ordered the queen.

This terrified me, and Umpin, too. I knew that royal dungeons were deep and damp and cold, and I'd heard that lions sometimes lurked in them.

The four newts grabbed hold of Umpin. At that moment he looked up at me with mournful blueberry eyes and said:

'You must try to save me.'

But I was just as scared of the naked queen as he was. I thought Prince Garamond might have said something as Umpin was being led away to the dungeon. The next moment the queen was pointing at me.

'And what's this?' she asked severely.

'This is my good friend from the forest,' said Garamond. 'His name is Prince Gregory Peggory.'

'Really?' said the queen. 'Haven't I told you that you're not to play with the Peggory princes?'

'But Mother,' said Garamond, 'this Peggory prince has saved my life a thousand times.'

His mother stood looking at the prince. Suddenly she began to shiver as if her shoulders were chilly. I thought that maybe it was her own wickedness that was making her so cold. 'Darling boy,' she said at last. 'I don't know what's come over me today. But this Peggory prince may dine at the castle.'

'Thanks a lot, Your Majesty,' I said before she had time to change her mind.

'NEWTS!' shouted the queen.

6

The Ballroom

The doors were immediately flung open, and the four newts entered.

'Conduct this Peggory prince to the ballroom at once,' said the queen. 'I command that ample quantities of pancakes and jam be served. But first, everyone must eat a plateful of alphabet biscuits.'

The newts approached me, and it was a bit of a scary moment even though I wasn't going to be thrown into the dungeon.

They led me to a large room where a table was already being laid for four.

Soon the royal family arrived. First came the

queen herself. She glided
across the room and seated
herself on the opposite
side of the table. Next
came Garamond, who
sat next to me. Finally,
a small girl came
tripping into the ballroom:
it was Flora. I thought it
strange that she'd come
all the way up from the south.

The queen clapped her hands.

'All rise for Princess Aurora,' she said.

We all stood up, and Flora sat down next to the
queen.

The princess was barefoot, just like me. She
hadn't managed to change into royal garments,
either; she was still wearing her nightie. But
Flora's nightie was so special that it could easily
be worn at other times too. She would flutter
about in her nightie all day long when the
weather was hot.

'Flora!' I whispered.

She looked down at the floor.

'Young Prince Peggory,' said the queen, 'I don't
think you can have heard what I said a moment
ago. I said that the princess's name is Aurora.

And that's not the same thing at all as sharing a name with some common little girl from the south.'

I must have made a mistake. The princess couldn't be Flora after all. We'd always been good friends, and she'd never have lied and made me look stupid in front of the entire castle.

Even so I said:

'Why are you wearing my cousin's nightie?'

I knew immediately I'd said something wrong. So did the queen. She turned really severe at this. She stood up and announced:

'It is with deep regret that I now perceive Gregory Peggory is a villain of the worst kind. And my regret is very nearly as deep as the dungeon. Never before has anyone called Princess Aurora a thief, nor described her loveliest dress as a nightie.'

'That's certainly true,' Prince Garamond put in. 'On the other hand, he's fitted together some important pieces in a very large jigsaw, so he shouldn't be cast into the dungeon just yet. But he's only got one chance left.'

My head was swimming, but I made up my mind from now on to be very careful with anything to do with words.

'Newts!' shouted the queen.

'Serve the alphabet biscuits at once!'

One of the newts opened a wide door at one end of the ballroom – and in came four small cardboard cars, each driven by its own engine. They were all loaded with alphabet biscuits. On reaching the centre of the room, they went their

separate ways, until one was parked under each of the four chairs. Now they had only to be lifted on to the table, and this the newts did.

We opened up the cars and spread our portions on the white tablecloth in front of us. I made sure I did everything slightly after the others so I wouldn't make any mistakes.

It was harder than I'd feared, because now the queen ordered us not to eat our alphabet biscuits until we'd formed them into words. I wasn't very good at reading, however, and found writing even more difficult.

The others wrote lots of funny words with their letters. QUEEN JELLY, CASTLE BALCONY, CHAMBERLAIN, BOTTLE POST, HYPNOSIS, GOOSEBERRY, FROGMAN ... They read out everything they'd written before putting the biscuits into their mouths. I didn't say a word. I just sat there fingering my biscuits.

When the queen realised that something was amiss with me, she leapt up from her chair.

'Doesn't the Peggory prince like the queen's biscuits?' she asked, pointing at me as if I'd just pulled a face at her, which I hadn't.

'I'm sorry, I'm not good at reading letters,' I said, melting with embarrassment.

'Did you hear that, Aurora?' she roared. 'This Peggory prince says he can't read!'

'But the princess is a whole year older than me and she's been going to school much longer,' I said.

'Nonsense! No one goes to school here. But if you don't make some words out of your letters right this minute we'll take away your powers of speech as well. And Peggory princes who haven't learnt to speak get thrown into the dungeon immediately. I read that in a very old book. Is that understood?'

'Yes!' I said as clearly as I could.

Deep down I was glad the queen had spelt out exactly what would happen if I didn't make some words out of the letters lying on the tablecloth before me. For now I knew I had to try.

I arranged all the letters in lines. Then I read out: 'THANK YOU TO THE QUEEN AND HER DAUGHTER THE PRINCESS FOR LETTING ME VISIT THE CASTLE.' It was the politest thing I could think of to say.

'Will you see if he's read it correctly?' the queen asked Garamond.

And the prince, whom I'd saved from bewitchment as a frog earlier in the day, leant over and read out:

'GMARSK SVIBYLL WARUX SIB
MALGHEP QUIBUX RATAMURLOW
HEXATURP THE KING'S HEART.'
I wasn't particularly scared any longer, as I knew
now that I was bound for the dungeon. But I felt a
bit foolish writing all those stupid words.

'He's abused my precious letters by writing a
load of rot and rubbish!' said the queen, waving
her arms about.

Just then one of the newts came up to the table
and interrupted the conversation.

'Gracious queen!' he began. 'I feel compelled to
inform Your Majesty that this Peggory prince
hasn't written a load of rot and rubbish. Every

word he's put down is in boggart language.'

'Then he's a spy!' exclaimed the queen.

I thought she was quite right, I felt just like a spy.

'But what does it *mean?*' she screamed. 'Is there no one here who can read boggart language?'

'I'll translate, with the queen's permission,' said the newt. 'It says: "THANK YOU TO THE QUEEN AND HER DAUGHTER THE PRINCESS FOR LETTING ME VISIT THE CASTLE".'

But I'd said that already, so I couldn't see the point of his translation.

The queen rose and tapped her glass with a fork.

'In that case, since the Peggory prince can read and write, even if it is only in boggart language, he can keep his powers of speech. Being the boggarts' spy in the castle is a more serious matter. But that can wait until tomorrow morning. It's time for the main course.'

'Hooray!' yelled Her Highness Princess Aurora.

I wasn't quite sure whether she said it because I wasn't going to be turned into lion-fodder, or because she would soon be eating pancakes. But Flora always shouted hooray when her mum gave her pancakes. So this princess would certainly do likewise, I thought, because everybody likes pancakes.

7

The King's Heart

A large dish of piping hot waffles was wheeled into the ballroom on a trolley. Next to the waffles was a jam-dish.

'But, Mummy,' Princess Aurora exclaimed, 'I thought you said we were having pancakes?'

'Well, there was a last-minute change,' replied her queen mother. 'It's not fitting to eat pancakes and strawberry jam when the king's heart has been stolen.'

'But I *want* pancakes,' Aurora whined.

'Be quiet, Flora!' scolded the queen.

She'd given the game away. Now I knew that it really was my cousin, but that she'd been turned into a princess by the wicked queen.

'Both are made with the same batter,' the queen went on. 'I've told you that time and time again. It's the same with frogs and tadpoles. They look different, but they're made of the same stuff.'

As she made this last remark, I glanced at the jam on the table. At first I'd imagined it was gooseberry jam, but now I realised it was frogspawn, otherwise why would the queen suddenly start talking about frogs and tadpoles?

I attempted to fool them like I had with the alphabet biscuits. I helped myself to two waffle-hearts and pressed them together without a single morsel of frogspawn in between.

'Gregory Peggory! Why aren't you eating the castle's gooseberry jam?' cried the queen.

'I'm allergic,' I said.

'Rubbish! That's just something people say when they don't want to eat what's put in front of them.'

I didn't dare do anything except spread some frogspawn between the two waffle-hearts. I could have been mistaken.

But I wasn't. I could taste straight away that this jam wasn't made from gooseberries, but had been fished up from the Newt Pond below the castle. I'd never eaten frogspawn before, but you can tell what some foods taste like just by looking at them.

Suddenly Princess Aurora stood up and pointed to the alphabet biscuits which were still lying on the table just as I'd left them.

'Mummy,' she said to her queen mother, 'the alphabet biscuits don't spell out what that newt said.'

The newts, who'd been standing at attention along the walls, turned and looked at one another.

'But Princess Aurora, dear,' said the queen, 'you can't read boggart language.'

'Yes I can,' said Princess Aurora, and the newts began pacing up and down the room. 'When I was small, I often played with the Peggory princes in the forest, and I learnt boggart language too. Children pick up new languages much quicker than adults, you know.'

'What does it say, then?' asked the queen.

'It says: "SECRET MESSAGE TO EVERYONE IN THE CASTLE: IT WAS THE NEWTS WHO STOLE THE KING'S HEART".'

Several of the newts ran out of the ballroom, but quickly returned, bringing lots of other newts with them.

The queen rose from her seat.

'Newts!' she shouted. 'I command you to round up all the newts and throw them into the dungeon without delay.'

And they really did begin to take each other prisoner. In the end they'd all been caught. They were standing in a tight huddle in one corner with their arms clasped round each other.

Suddenly, a fat frog sprang out from among them. It began leaping about on the floor.

'There's the king's heart,' screamed the queen, pointing down at the frog. 'Quickly, Garamond! You must save the king's heart!'

But he didn't get the chance, because just then the newts struggled out of one another's clutches and overpowered the prince, the princess and the

queen. They tied them up with a stout rope and dragged them out of the ballroom.

I was left alone in the great room. The frog-heart sat on the floor puffing itself up and down, up and down. When I moved a bit closer, it began to hop around the room, but I kept running after the poor frog until I managed to catch it in my hands.

I clutched the king's heart tight to my chest and tiptoed out of the ballroom. In the long corridor outside I heard something rattling on the floor above. I could feel how the moist frog-heart kept on beating and beating.

It didn't take me long to find the room where the king lay on his red silk bed, in exactly the same position as I'd seen him before. I placed the moist heart under his red cape. Just then, his eyelids began to flutter.

'Heartfelt returns, Your Majesty!' I said bowing.

He gave a couple of heavy sighs and looked up at me.

'I do believe you've brought me back to life again, my good Peggory prince,' he said.

I told him about everything that had happened at the castle. Then the king made a speech.

'Gregory Peggory,' he began. 'Your arrival here at the castle has been a great boon. Your secret writing has exposed the newts as heartless thieves. Once you've got the king's heart you're well on the way to getting his kingdom, too, so they probably had plans to steal it. I've always known that newts survive by eating frogspawn. But eating frogspawn is no better than eating tadpoles, and eating tadpoles is the same as eating live frogs. Do you see, Gregory Peggory? And we all know, too, that anyone who eats frogs is really eating bewitched princes, and someone who eats bewitched princes is eating the king's own flesh and blood.'

I thought this a very serious speech, especially serious as it ended with the word 'blood'.

When he'd finished his speech he said:

'Come with me, brave Peggory prince. We'll make our way to the dungeon and release the boggart Umpin as a thank-you for making so many pancakes and jam, with strawberries from his own garden.'

8

The Tower

It was a long way through the corridors of the castle to the dungeon. The king was so tired that he couldn't run. My legs ached a bit as well.

'An old man and a young boy are like two brothers,' he said as we walked along.

I looked up at him. I didn't know what he meant.

'The boy's strength grows year by year,' he went on. 'And the old man's fades. But right now we're both equal in strength. So it's very convenient to be walking together.'

Suddenly a clock began to chime. 'Ding-dong ... ding-dong ... '

I counted ten strokes.

'That's the castle clock,' said the king solemnly. 'Each hour it reminds us that time is passing.'

He laid his hand on my head and continued:

'But, in reality it's not *time* that's passing, my boy.'

'Isn't it?'

'It's us. Without people, time would have no hands.'

'So what does time do, then?' I asked.

'Time heals all wounds. And time opens up more.'

'So time is both good and bad,' I said.

'Both, yes.'

Shortly afterwards he stopped at a rusty iron door, revealing some stairs that led down into the cellar. The door creaked as it swung back. Then I took the kind king's hand.

The stairs were so dark that we had to feel our way down. We soon found ourselves in the cellar, and now it was a little easier to see because our eyes had got used to the dark. The floor was strewn with lots of old clocks. Some were covered with dust and cobwebs. There was a smell of damp and decay.

'Here time stands almost completely still,' said the king.

He'd hardly finished before one of the clocks
started ticking.

'Almost completely still,' the king repeated.
'Because it's possible to hide from time. Someone
who plays hide-and-seek with time is only playing
hide-and-seek with himself.'

I tried to think through all the wise things the
kind king had said. I'd once heard someone say
that time plods on and on but never arrives at the
door. Now I understood the point of the riddle.
Time doesn't move forwards or
backwards, or up or down. Time
moves in a completely different
way.

'Stop!' shouted the king
suddenly. I crept close to him.

He pointed down at a
large hole in the floor.

There was no railing
round it. I realised it must
be the dungeon.

Soon we could hear
Umpin the boggart
groaning. I lay down on my
stomach and peered into
the dark. A cold draught hit
my face.

Far, far below I spied my
good friend. But I couldn't
see any lions down there.
The only animals that
scurried about in the half-
light were a few playful rats.

The kind king found a stout rope which he lowered into the depths. Suddenly it went taut, and the next moment Umpin came clambering up out of the abyss. He had to shake off the rats before he could stand upright.

'Aren't you His Majesty the king?' he asked, awestruck.

The king coughed twice. 'You're not seeing things, my dear Umpin. This brave Peggory prince has snatched back my heart from the thieves who'd stolen it, and those thieves were the newts.'

'The newts?' exclaimed the boggart. 'Was it really the newts who made off with the king's heart?'

The king nodded.

'In that case they've probably carried off the child of your heart as well,' continued Umpin. 'I mean Princess Aurora. If I'm not very much mistaken, she'll be trussed up in some really high tower. I read about it once in a very old book.'

We realised we had to hurry to the high tower. We tiptoed past all the old clocks and rushed up the stairs to the rusty iron door.

Eight fat newts were lined up in the corridor outside.

'Greetings, my dear newts,' the king said in a friendly tone. 'Would you be kind enough to let us pass?'

'We're sorry,' said the largest of them, 'but no one is allowed to go a single step further. We are in control of the castle now.'

The king was so sad he didn't know what to say.

'How could you be so disobedient?' he asked at length. 'I was the one who fished you all up from the misery of the cold Newt Pond down there. Here, in the castle, you've been dry and well looked after. So, I command you, let us past so that we can rescue Princess Aurora.'

The newt shook his head.

'From now on, we're only taking orders from the queen, but we've hidden her down a secret well so we don't have to listen to all her scolding.'

He tried to push us down into the cellar again, but I darted forward and shot between his legs. Two or three newts came galumphing after me, and one of them threw a spear which struck the wall just above my head and lodged there, vibrating. But I had to rescue the princess, and soon I'd shaken off all the newts just as Umpin had shaken off the rats when he climbed out of the dungeon.

I had no idea of the way to the tower, but I decided to head upwards each time I came to some stairs. Finally, I found myself mounting a tight spiral staircase. The stairs led to a small tower room, and in the middle of the room stood a cage.

The cage was just big enough to take the princess. If I hadn't got there in time, she would certainly soon have died for lack of space, I thought, because princesses are still growing.

She was lying perfectly still and looked as if she was asleep. In the half-darkness her golden hair fell like shafts of sunlight across her face.

'Aurora,' I whispered gently. 'I've come from the depths to rescue you.'

As soon as I said this, she sat up as far as she could, but that was not very far. The cage was hardly bigger than a birdcage.

'I knew you'd find me in the end,' she said plaintively.

I remembered how Flora had once said something like that when we'd been playing hide-and-seek at her house. After seeking and seeking all morning, I'd finally found her hiding in the shed.

Now I saw that the cage was fastened with a strong padlock.

'You must try your key and see if it fits,' said the princess.

She reached out through the bars and tugged at something hanging round my neck on a string.

I touched it with my hand and felt the key to my house. I pulled it over my head and tried it in the padlock. To my amazement, the keyhole in the padlock exactly fitted my key.

The princess laughed with delight as I pulled her out of the cage. But suddenly we caught the sound of shuffling footsteps on the stairs, and she stopped laughing.

'The newts!' she whispered.

I quickly hid the princess behind the door and then opened a large window in the tower just as two newts came clumping into the room. When one of them attempted to catch me, I sidestepped deftly and the newt went tumbling out of the window and down into the castle yard all those storeys below. I heard the clatter as he hit the ground.

The other one tried to push me into the cage, but I twisted like a snake, and it was the newt who ended up in the cage, not me. I dived down and turned the key in the padlock.

The newt roared and wailed, so I got down on my hands and knees and peered into the cage.

'You should treat others as you'd like them to treat you,' I said. 'You wanted to put me in the cage, so it's only fair that I should do the same to you.'

'Let me out, you stupid Peggory-person,' he said.

I thought for a moment. Then I said:

'You can choose whether to stay there or follow your friend out of the window.'

His only reply was a few grunting noises, but I could tell they meant he'd rather stay in the cage. I dropped the key of the padlock on the floor. At least the poor newt could have the pleasure of *looking* at the key to freedom.

Then Aurora came out of hiding.

9

Midsummer Bonfire

We crept down the stairs from the high tower. Luckily, we didn't encounter any newts in this confined space where there weren't any windows to throw them out of, or any cages to lock them into.

'Where's the secret well?' I asked.

As I spoke I began to think of Flora's well down south, just behind her house. Sometimes we'd lift the cover and drop big stones down into the well, though we knew we weren't allowed to. Once when Grandad was there on a visit, Flora's mum caught us red-handed. We were sent to bed without any supper. 'Straight to bed!' she shouted after us. Even Grandad thought it a fair punishment, and that was the worst punishment of all. That night I cried myself to sleep.

The princess looked up at me with a surprised expression as if we'd talked about secret wells many times before. But I told her that the newts had hidden the queen in a secret well so they wouldn't have to listen to all her scolding.

By the time she'd replied we were in the yard in front of the castle.

'There are lots of wells in the king's garden,' she said. 'It won't be easy finding the right one.'

We ran in to the biggest garden I'd ever seen. There were red deck-chairs everywhere. The huge frogs hopped about amongst the trees and deck-chairs, grazing the green grass. At first I was a little nervous of them, but the princess told me they weren't dangerous.

'They've only got one bad habit, they're so fond of children that they like jumping up and licking their faces.'

No sooner had she spoken than two frogs came bounding towards us and began licking our faces as if we were frog-food.

'Down!' commanded Princess Aurora, and at that they slunk away and crouched under the trees again.

62

The first well we peered into had nothing but tadpoles in it. The next well looked very secret indeed, because it was hidden behind some thick bushes. There was no queen there, either, but so many jumping fish that the princess and I got our feet splashed with water.

To get to the third well we had to cross a field of grass tall enough to tickle our noses. I thought we were going to drown in the grass.

Soon we heard a nasty grunting noise, and the next moment we spied another well. We stooped over it and peered down. All the water had been pumped out, but on the big stones at the bottom sat the queen and Prince Garamond. They were bound hand and foot, and they had scarves in their mouths so they couldn't call for help.

'Gmrf . . . gmobf,' said the queen when she caught sight of us.

I began wondering how we could haul them out of the well. Then I had an idea.

'You're very like someone I know called Flora,' I said to Aurora. 'And she's got a skipping rope that's so long it's called a dangly-rope . . . '

I didn't need to say any more, because Aurora was already setting off at a run through the tall grass. I lay down flat and looked down at the captives.

'Gmrf . . . gmobf,' said the queen again.

Soon Aurora was back with the dangly-rope. We threw one end down the well, but it just hung there and nothing happened. That was because the queen and prince were tied hand and foot.

'I'll have to climb down and rescue them,' I said.

Aurora grasped the skipping rope with both hands, while I began to climb down into the well. When I'd got to the bottom, I gazed up. Far above I could make out a small, round sky. And from it hung the angel-hair belonging to the princess, who was lying on her tummy gazing down.

I quickly loosened the rope that was tied tightly round the prince's wrists. Then he pulled the scarf out of his mouth and said:

'Climbing down to us was a brave thing to do, but how are we to get up again?'

He undid the rope round his feet and then set his mother free.

'Can't you see the princess up there?' I said.

Garamond shook his head.

'How can a small princess haul a big queen out of a deep well?'

'She could haul me up first, couldn't she?' I said. 'Once I'm up, she and I could pull the rope for you, and then all three of us can haul out the queen.'

The prince turned up his nose at
the idea, but he knew we had to
give it a try.

'You must take a firm grip of
the rope with both hands and
pull me up!' I called out to
Aurora.

I grasped the rope tightly.
All went well to begin with,
but when I was almost half
way, it suddenly got too
much for the princess.
I slid down into the
well again. Aurora
almost fell down
into it too.

'Tut!' said the queen irritably. 'This really is no time for playing tug-of-war.'

She said this even before she knew if I'd hurt myself.

I thought of how Grandad used to haul his boat out of the water.

'Try running the rope round a tree,' I called up to the princess.

Soon she was able to pull me out of the well. Then Aurora and I hauled the rope for the prince together. It didn't take long before he was up. That only left the queen. We lay flat, all three of us, peering down at her.

'Get me out of here immediately!' she commanded.

We dropped the dangly-rope down to her and hauled the queen out of the well. She was very heavy.

'Now we must release the king and Umpin the boggart from the curse of the newts!' said Garamond. He drew his sword from its sheath. 'To the castle yard!' he cried.

We went through the tall grass, and ran so quickly across the king's garden that the frogs began croaking all at once.

The newts had lit a great midsummer bonfire in the castle yard. Just as we got there, Umpin and the kind king were being carried down the steps from the castle.

'They're going to burn us on the bonfire!' Umpin shouted.

The prince rushed at the newts, but before he could use his sword the soldiers stormed up and overpowered him.

'Newts!' shouted the queen. 'This is the limit. I told you a long time ago to get into the dungeon, didn't I?'

With that, all preparations for the midsummer bonfire ceased. The newts released the king and the prince and Umpin immediately. Some even began pouring water on the fire. In the end they just stood looking shamefacedly at the angry queen.

'Off to the dungeon with you!' she went on. 'No ifs and buts. That's all the fun and games for now!'

They lined up straight away. It was a joy to see how obedient they were.

The newts began to march up the steps of the castle in an orderly line. I was curious to know if they really would do exactly as the queen told them, so I followed at a safe distance.

At last we arrived in the dungeon. One by one the newts jumped into the hideous hole. The noise

as each one hit the bottom reverberated round the cellar.

Finally, the very last newt jumped into the abyss, and I was left alone in the cellar. I lay flat on my tummy and peered down.

'Now you've got what you deserved,' I said. 'You've all been so wicked that we just can't have newts like you in the castle.'

Just then I felt I needed a pee. I hadn't been for a really long time and I stood on the edge of the

hole and peed and peed into the dungeon.

No sooner had silence fallen in the cellar than I heard something thumping. At first I thought it was my heart, but then I realised it was one of the old clocks that had suddenly begun to tick again.

I groped my way back to the stairs. Just as I put my foot on the first step, something leaped out of a large clock that was covered in a thick layer of dust and cobwebs. 'Cuckoo!' it said.

It was only a cuckoo clock.

I raced up the stairs and past the iron door. When I got out into the castle yard, I found it was like a huge pool. A great deal of water had been used to put out the newts' bonfire. My feet got a soaking as I waded through the warm water.

10

The High Chair

In the king's garden, the king and queen and the prince and princess were seated round a large table which had been brought out specially for the occasion. As I walked towards them I noticed that everything had been arranged for a summer evening barbecue.

Grandad had been brilliant at barbecuing. I only wished he could have enjoyed the evening with me. He had died suddenly of a heart attack while Mum was on holiday at a castle in France. I was staying in my grandparents' house and had just gone into the living room to give Grandad his usual goodnight hug. He lay on the red sofa and didn't make any movement when I put my arm round his neck and squeezed him to me. At first I thought he was only resting, but he didn't answer when I spoke to him, so I called Grandma. Later that evening I realised he was dead.

Luckily, I didn't have to dwell on these thoughts, because all the royal family were waving to me and saying that we were going to have a nice time even though it was late and children should have been in bed long ago.

Umpin was sitting at the table as well. Also present was a stiff man in a very splendid uniform.

'Gregory Peggory!' said the kind king. 'May I introduce the lord chamberlain of the castle.'

The stiff man in the blue uniform rose immediately and clicked his heels together, at the same time lifting his hand to his brow in a rigid salute.

'I'm very pleased to meet you,' I said as formally as I could. I had never met a lord chamberlain before, but I knew perfectly well you couldn't just say 'hi' or 'hello' to people like that, because a lord chamberlain was the most noble person in the entire kingdom.

'The pleasure is entirely mine,' was all he said.

He sat down again, and the king tapped his glass with a pen.

'Now that this castle is rid of the newts,' he said, 'it's fitting we should dine on barbecued frogs' legs. I've already put some juicy ones on the menu.'

He pointed down at a large barbecue.

I couldn't make head or tail of this. After all, the king had said that eating anything to do with frogs was like consuming the king's own flesh and blood. But I'd already attended one formal meal here at the castle, and that hadn't been a great success, so I didn't dare protest.

'I protest!' cried the lord chamberlain, as he rose and pointed down at me with a long, quivering index finger. 'This Peggory prince was just thinking that he didn't want to eat the food we dish up at the castle.'

I glanced despairingly round the table. Everyone was suddenly looking so sad and serious.

The queen shook her head vigorously. She hadn't even bothered to wrap a shawl round her shoulders, even though it had begun to turn quite chilly.

The lord chamberlain spoke again. 'Now he's sitting there rueing the fact that the queen hasn't got dressed up!'

I decided not to think any more thoughts for a while, but just then the queen said:

'I think we need to explain why we have employed a lord chamberlain here at the castle. He doesn't just read through all the letters, he reads people's thoughts as well, because all wickedness starts in the mind.'

I could see the battle was lost. It takes a lot of practice to control what goes on inside your head, I thought. Not saying bad things is much easier.

'Bad things,' said the lord chamberlain, 'always begin here.'

75

He leant over the table and prodded my forehead.

I looked up at the kind king, but even he seemed deadly earnest.

'My good Peggory prince,' he said. 'The queen has decreed that it's not enough just to sit quietly at the table. If a prince wants to do well here at the castle, he must also learn to control his innermost thoughts.'

The queen and the lord chamberlain nodded sternly. But Umpin the boggart now rose and tapped his glass.

'Your Royal Highnesses,' he began. 'Of course it can be a boon if everyone is pure in word, thought and deed. But you must be allowed to practise one thing at a time, provided you're sitting nicely at the table. This Peggory prince should learn to control his thoughts like everyone else, but he can't be held responsible for everything that goes on at the castle.'

The queen's expression began to turn ugly, and she drummed the table with her fingers.

'Do you really mean to say that Gregory Peggory should be allowed to sit here thinking the queen looks ugly?' the lord chamberlain asked. 'And what she does with her fingers is entirely her own business as well.'

'It's hardly surprising that a poor forest prince should be a bit confused when such a lot of strange things are being said,' Umpin went on. 'An entire castle is too much for a small boy to cope with.'

The queen rose from her seat and leant over the table. Then she pointed at Umpin and me.

'Pah!' she exclaimed. 'I'm beginning to lose patience with all this nonsense. We can solve this problem quite easily by throwing this Peggory prince and this Umpin boggart into the dungeon right this minute. I've always said sprogs weren't welcome here.'

There was an intense hush round the table. Only Princess Aurora seemed not to notice. She went to the barbecue and took a frog's leg which she licked quietly, instead of looking cross like the others.

The king tapped his glass with his pen.

'My dear queen,' he began. 'I must insist that justice prevail here in my castle. Therefore, neither Umpin the boggart nor Gregory Peggory may be cast into the dungeon before they've been tried by a court of law. Lord Chamberlain, you know what to do.'

The lord chamberlain rose and clicked his heels, then disappeared up the steps into the castle. Soon he returned carrying a very tall chair.

He placed the chair on the grass in front of the assembled company and climbed up on to it. Now he was sitting well above the rest of us.

'This is the castle's highest high chair,' the lord chamberlain began. 'If there be any in this company who have complaint to make against the boggart, Umpin, or his friend Gregory Peggory, let her speak now.'

The queen began to mince up and down as if the lord chamberlain was a lifeguard and the whole world one huge seaside.

'I really shouldn't need to say this,' she began. 'But no one can have failed to notice all the unpleasantness we've suffered here at the castle since this Peggory prince arrived.'

'That's no proof, Your Majesty,' Umpin ventured. 'It must be proved that it's the Peggory prince's fault that things have been unpleasant at the castle.'

'Fine!' the queen went on. 'In that case, I'll begin by asking Gregory Peggory if he thinks I'm a total nitwit.'

'Not at all, Your Majesty,' I blurted out before stopping to think about it. But then I did think about it, and I thought that I did think she was a total nitwit and not only that, but that she was nasty and horrible into the bargain.

'Lord Chamberlain!' cried the queen. 'Would you be so kind as to read the Peggory prince's thoughts?'

The lord chamberlain looked down first at me and then at the queen.

'He thought that the queen is a total nitwit and that she's nasty and horrible into the bargain,' said the lord chamberlain.

'Thank you!' said the queen. 'So I've proved that Gregory Peggory tells lies. And those who lie, steal. And those who steal are thrown into the dungeon without delay.'

That sounded quite reasonable to me, so I merely looked down at the grass. But I did think the prince or princess might have said something to save me, since I'd saved them several times already.

The princess merely sucked away at her frog's leg, just like Flora and her chicken leg that time Mum got cross with me for wetting my pants, even though it had only happened because Flora had said something so funny that I almost died laughing. She was a cowardy-custard as far as I was concerned.

'Now this Peggory prince is thinking the princess is a cowardy-custard,' the lord chamberlain reported.

'That's perfectly possible,' Umpin put in, 'and perhaps he's right. But what isn't right is to condemn Gregory Peggory for thinking the queen's a nitwit before we have looked at whether it's true.'

The queen straightened up and pointed at my good friend.

'Proof!' she screamed.

'This wicked queen once accused me of stealing the king's heart,' Umpin began. 'And I was thrown into the dungeon, too. But everyone knows it was the newts who committed the crime. And who was in charge of the newts? It was the queen, so it was she who stole the king's heart, and so it's true that the queen is a total nitwit who's also nasty and horrible.'

At this the king got up from his chair.

'This has been a sad day in every respect,' he began. 'For either my beloved queen has suddenly been turned into a nasty, horrible nitwit, or my good Prince Peggory of the Forest is a spy, a liar and a thief. It's impossible for me to judge which of them is right.'

'I suggest that we hand the decision over to the lord chamberlain at once,' said the queen.

'Unfair!' I shouted angrily. 'It's unfair to let the lord chamberlain decide. He always sides with the queen.'

But it didn't matter what I thought. The lord chamberlain sat up in his judgement-seat and said:

'Prince Gregory Peggory of the Forest and Umpin the boggart of the same place, you are both hereby condemned to be cast into the dungeon immediately after dinner.'

11

The Dungeon

Several times I'd had the feeling that my visit to the
castle would end up with the queen throwing me
into the dungeon. And now, as the lord
chamberlain announced the fact loud and clear,
I began to cry.

It didn't help in the slightest. Even though
the tears were streaming down my cheeks,
nobody at the castle showed any sign of wanting to
comfort me. Quite the opposite – they all went
over to the barbecue and helped themselves to the
frogs' legs. I sat there sobbing on my own until
I saw Princess Aurora begin playing with a
yo-yo right in front of me, as if nothing had

happened. That made me so angry that I stopped crying immediately.

'You'd do better getting your mum some clothes, than behaving like a street urchin,' I said.

I could say whatever I wanted now; I'd been condemned to the dungeon anyway.

In fact, I was already quite used to thinking about sad things. After Grandad died, there were many things to be sad about in my family.

It all began when Mum wanted to go off to the castle in France, but I wasn't allowed to go too, even though I pestered her for weeks.

It was only when Grandad's heart suddenly stopped that Mum broke off her holiday and took the first plane home so that she'd at least get back in time for the funeral.

I loved Grandad so much, because he always tossed me high up in the air and said I was his little prince. But now Grandad was east of the sun and west of the moon. At least, he wasn't here any more, and that was awful. I missed him terribly. I thought it was unfair that a nice man couldn't be in charge of the barbecue just because his heart wouldn't beat.

I began to mull all this over now that the queen had decided to throw me into the dungeon. I kept on hoping she would change her mind, but this time she didn't start to shiver or feel cold.

'Forgive me for interrupting the festivities,' said the lord chamberlain after a while. 'I'd just like to know if we're to throw these ne'er-do-wells into the dungeon before or after pudding.'

'The sooner the better,' exclaimed the queen. 'I can't abide sprogs under my feet all day.'

Umpin and I looked imploringly at the kind king.

'Must I be thrown into the dungeon?' I asked.

'Unfortunately, my good Peggory prince, even you must do what the queen of the castle commands,' said the king, clearing his throat and looking at the queen.

'Your Majesty, why do you say these things when you're not wicked like the queen?' asked the boggart, drawing himself up.

Then the king said something that stayed in my mind for a long while afterwards.

'I'm not so wicked, my dear Umpin, but since my heart was stolen by these French newts, I'm not as powerful as I was.'

Hearing that the newts were French made me start. Even though I hadn't realised it clearly, and had never been to France, I'd always had the feeling that was where the newts came from.

It wasn't a long farewell. As there were no more newts in the castle to deal with people like Umpin and me, the queen herself, accompanied by the lord chamberlain, conducted us to the big hole in the cellar into which we were to be thrown.

I only remember turning and waving to the rest of the company in the garden, but apart from the kind king with the weak heart, nobody waved back. The spoilt princess played with her stupid yo-yo as if nothing sad was about to happen,

while
Prince
Garamond
sat in the
evening sun lazily
cleaning his nails with
his sword.

'Come along, now,' said
the queen, prodding Umpin
and me up the steps to the castle.
'We really can't spend the whole of

this lovely June
evening getting rid
of you two.'

Soon we found
ourselves down in
the dark cellar with
all the old clocks.
The queen and the
lord chamberlain
pushed us into the
hole.

We fell and fell,
down and down.
The dungeon was so
deep it took a long
time before we
stopped falling.

I remember
shouting: 'We're
falling!'

'We are indeed,
Gregory Peggory,'
replied Umpin in
mid-air. 'But luckily
we haven't reached
the bottom yet.'

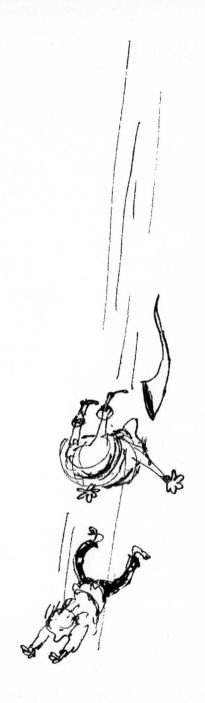

Something must have broken our fall at the last moment, for we didn't get so much as a graze when we landed.

When we got to our feet, we heard a voice from way, way above us.

'Now you've got what you deserve. You've both been very silly. We just can't have Peggory princes and boggarts like you in the castle.'

The last thing we heard from overhead was the lord chamberlain's cruel laughter.

12

The
Dark Cauldron

'Now we really are in a fine state, Gregory
Peggory,' said Umpin as he dusted his green
coat.

I couldn't see how anyone could be in a fine
state in a dungeon. It also began to dawn on me
that we were now in the same place as all the
newts who'd been thrown in. They'd certainly
wreak an awful revenge.

We'd fallen through total darkness, but it wasn't
pitch black at the bottom of the dungeon.

'It's the glow-worms shining in the dark,' said
Umpin.

He pointed down at rows of tiny luminous

creatures, hardly bigger than tadpoles.

'Are there glow-worms here?' I asked in surprise.

'Do you really mean to tell me you don't know where these luminous worms come from, Gregory Peggory?' said Umpin.

I shook my head in shame.

'They're transformed newts,' he explained. 'Once the newts get old enough to light a great midsummer bonfire to roast the king and his family, they always get cast into the castle dungeon, where they're immediately turned into glow-worms to light up the dark for Peggory princes. I read about it in an old book.'

I thought the whole thing sounded very odd.

'Do they ever turn back into newts?' I wanted to know.

'You clearly don't dip into old books very much, my young Peggory prince. It says that the glow-worms immediately embark on the long journey back to the Newt Pond from which they once emerged. Only when they arrive there in late autumn will they become newts again, and can again be turned into castle guards by wicked queens who are on the lookout for French newts.'

'How can they get back to the Newt Pond – or all the way to France – if they're trapped in a deep hole?' I had to ask.

'This dungeon isn't quite what it seems,' Umpin went on. 'If I'm not mistaken, we're now standing deep in an underground valley, and this valley leads right down to the Newt Pond. Can't you see that river running just there? The water in it comes from the wells in the king's garden.'

No sooner had he said these words than I looked about me and discovered we were indeed standing on the bank of an underground river. The light from the glow-worms – which were crawling incredibly slowly along the river-bank – meant that we weren't left completely in the dark down there.

I realised it would take a very long time before these luminous worms managed to turn into newts again. I also felt very relieved that I wouldn't have to spend the rest of my life in a dungeon, because if the glow-worms could crawl all the way back to the Newt Pond, we could surely do the same.

'Come with me, Gregory Peggory,' said Umpin, beckoning.

We began to follow the underground river. After walking a long while, the ground suddenly became so steep that the path petered out.

'We won't be able to go further on foot,' the boggart declared. 'From now on we must travel by water. There's a little boat down here.'

He pointed to a boat that was identical to the red rowing boat Grandad had owned.

We had to clamber down a steep hillside. It was

as much as I could do not to slip on the steep ground and fall into the water, but soon we were sitting opposite each other in the boat, exactly as Grandad and I had done so many times the summer before he died. Umpin didn't even need to row – the current took the boat of its own accord.

'Now, Gregory Peggory, we're in the deeps,' he

said, his voice making the underground cave reverberate. 'We're so deep down that only deep truths can be spoken here.'

But I had no deep truths to tell.

'We're deep beneath the surface, so we're not allowed to be as shallow as before,' continued the boggart.

I began to feel a bit scared about how the conversation would end if we started delving into things, so I said nothing.

'Do you know what these deeps are called?' whispered Umpin solemnly.

'Are they the deeps of death?' I asked, terrified. Everything seemed to be linked to my grandad.

'This is the Dark Cauldron,' said the boggart, looking out across the underground river.

'Is it really?'

Umpin nodded gravely, just like my grandad did when I asked him something serious.

'And soon the clock will strike eleven.'

He'd hardly finished speaking before he was pointing at the water. There I caught sight of an empty bottle with a cork in it. I leant over the side and lifted the bottle into the boat. It was then I realised it really was bottle-post, for inside the bottle was a piece of paper tied up with a pink silk ribbon.

I uncorked the bottle and pulled the message out. Inside the paper was a pair of glasses. As soon as I put them on, something wonderful happened. Even though I wasn't normally good at reading, with the glasses on I could read every word on the paper easily.

'I can read properly!' I shouted.

Umpin squinted up at me as if he was jealous.

'That's only because you've got a decent pair of reading glasses,' he said.

Then in a loud, clear voice I read out the contents of the note:

Dear Gregory Peggory,

I'm putting this message in a bottle, which I'll drop down one of the wells in the king's garden, to warn you and Umpin the boggart. The queen is planning to let out all the water from the wells so that it goes straight down into the dungeon and drowns you both. She's only waiting for the kind king to go and lie down on the sofa in the highest part of the castle. Then there will be a terrible flood in the Dark Cauldron. You must choose between blueberries and gooseberries.

Love, Princess Aurora.

'That queen is still set in her wicked ways,' sighed Umpin.

He put the oars into the rowlocks and rowed so that water spurted from the prow.

In the same instant we heard the entire underground valley booming to the sound of a roaring torrent. The flood-wave lifted us high into the air and didn't release us again until we were propelled out of the tunnel with water foaming all around us.

We might very easily have drowned. Instead, we floated down on to the Newt Pond. The boat didn't capsize, but it was practically full of water and both oars were missing.

We remained, drifting aimlessly in the middle of the big pond. All around us frogs croaked in the warm summer evening. Snakes and lizards crawled in the grass, and small birds chirped in the trees.

There were so many noises in the great forest that it sounded like a full orchestra.

When we finally drifted ashore near the place where, long, long ago, we'd caught all the tadpoles and kissed the frog who'd suddenly turned into a prince, we were both cold and wet.

Behind the Newt Pond we could see the castle towering into the evening sky. Ghastly noises could also be heard coming from that direction. I think it must have been the wicked queen screeching when she discovered we hadn't drowned after all.

Suddenly, there was a rustling in the grass. I saw that Umpin was getting frightened, and I began to feel frightened too. Then I saw one of the giant frogs crawling out of the water.

I felt my heart pounding twice as fast as usual. It was so close to my mouth that I was worried it might leap right out.

'We'll just have to get back to winter immediately!' Umpin exclaimed.

'Quite right,' I answered as quick as a flash. At the same moment we heard Princess Aurora calling out from the top of one of the castle's lofty towers:

'Beware the ways of wickedness!'

We looked at each other.

'You must take my hand, Gregory Peggory,' said Umpin.

And the next instant we were both standing on the frozen snow. All of a sudden I found myself wearing my nightclothes again, with all the pictures of cars and motorbikes, though one arm was torn because a frog had managed to cling to my jacket just as we were on our way out of one season and into another.

'They won't follow us here,' said Umpin breathlessly. 'Those are summertime dangers.'

13

Heartless

The great forest shone like silver, and above
the spruce trees the moon floated like a fat
balloon.

Now that all dangers were past, Umpin and I
paced up and down the frosty snow not knowing
what to say.

'Well, well . . . ' said the boggart finally, and then
repeated himself three times at least.

I realised this meant he wanted to say something
more to me, but didn't know where to begin. So I
said:

'My heart was in my mouth.'

Umpin peered up at me, and a tear formed in
the corner of each eye.

'It's better to have your heart in your mouth,

than to have no heart at all,' he said at last.

This answer troubled me. I began recalling what the prince had said about boggarts forever seeking a human heart. And how he'd added that the search goes on when the moon is full, and the snow hard.

'How can you be so certain you haven't got a heart?' I ventured.

He went on walking up and down for a while, then turned to me and said:

'Boggarts never have hearts, everyone knows that. But you can see for yourself if you like.'

I went up to him and put my ear close to his chest. It was as silent as a tomb inside.

'Then I don't understand how you can be alive,' I said. 'My grandad couldn't go on living when his heart stopped beating.'

Umpin drew himself up.

'Gregory Peggory,' he said, 'I don't have a heart that beats all the time because I'm not flesh and blood like you and all the frogs of the forest. And if I'm not flesh and blood, I must be a dream. But if I'm a dream, then there must be someone dreaming me and, if I'm not very much mistaken, that person is you.'

At this he dug his index finger into my chest so hard it almost hurt.

Now I was scared. If this
really was a dream, it was
the very first time I'd
entered into my dream
myself. And if the whole
of me had entered into the
dream, I wouldn't be in my
bed early tomorrow morning when
Mum or Dad came to wake me up. But then,
where would I be? It's hard enough searching
for a child who's got lost in a forest, I
thought, but finding one who's got lost
in a dream is even more difficult.
'That can't be true,' I
said, and now it was my
turn to have eyes
full of tears.

'It could be quite true, Gregory Peggory,' continued Umpin. 'It could, for instance, be as true as saying your grandad isn't alive any more, but he's still able to go on living in your thoughts.'

'That's not the same thing,' I said, 'and you're not to talk about my grandad, because you never sat on his lap and listened to fairy tales.'

Umpin thrust his arms behind his back and began wandering round and round on the crusted snow.

'I'm afraid it's precisely the same, my good Peggory prince,' he said. 'Neither I nor your grandad can run out into the fresh air and feel the sun on our faces like you can, for we are pure fantasy. And though I've never sat on your grandad's lap, or that of any other living person, I was present in many of the fairy tales he told you. Have you forgotten that your grandad told you stories about boggarts and princes and great white castles where exciting events are always unfolding?'

I couldn't deny that Grandad had told me all these things. But I still couldn't work out how Umpin was just a dream. He'd told me so many things I didn't know, and people in a dream could hardly be cleverer than the people who dreamed the dream.

I decided to test
this out a bit more.
The boggart was
still deep in
thought. Suddenly I
said:
'May I try to guess what
you're thinking?'
He looked surprised, but
nodded his head.
Now it was my turn to think. If
Umpin really was just part of my
dream, it shouldn't be too hard for me to
read his thoughts.

'I think you're thinking about pancakes,' I said.

'Wrong!' he replied pertly. 'I was just thinking
how good a nice glass of fruit juice would be.'

I was very pleased I'd guessed wrong, because
now I'd proved that Umpin wasn't a dream. Just to
make sure, I decided to ask him something else,
and it had to be so difficult that even I didn't know
the answer.

'What's the name of the highest mountain in the
world?' I asked.

'That's a very easy question, my good Peggory
prince. The mountain is called Galgeberg.'

I couldn't help laughing.

104

'That's very interesting,' I remarked. 'I didn't know that.'

Umpin began scratching his ears as if I'd said something that couldn't be right.

'You're living your own life, don't you see!' I cried as loudly as I could. 'And so you can't be my dream. And anyway, I'd never have bothered to dream about frogs and newts or wicked queens and mind-reading lord chamberlains if I'd had the choice.'

Umpin merely shook his head.

'You're a dear little prince, Gregory Peggory,' he said, 'but you're not always very wise.'

He pointed out across the forest and continued.

'There's a world out there,' he said. 'There are strange peoples and animals in it and many foreign lands. Are you saying that you know everything about the world out there?'

Now he sounded just like Grandad.

I shook my head, because I'd only ever visited England and Legoland, and there were still birds that came to our bird-table I didn't know the names of.

'Well, then,' Umpin continued. 'That's the outside world. But there's also a world within you, and that's called the world of fantasy. Are you saying you know everything about that world right down to the smallest detail?'

When he put it like that, I could hardly say yes. I just shook my head and looked sheepishly down at the snow.

'In that case, I don't think we should discuss it, or anything like it,' he proceeded. 'Instead, I think we should talk a bit about what it's like to have a heart. It's something all boggarts want to know.'

I wasn't sure how to answer him, but I felt my heart thumping in my chest. It leapt up and down, up and down just like a frog's heart.

'A heart goes on beating and beating,' the boggart went on. 'Isn't that rather strange? You don't even have to wind it up. And when you're asleep, or thinking about something completely different, your heart is doing its job even more accurately than a clock.'

Umpin peered up at me through half-closed eyes. Now I was certain the moment had come for him to steal my heart.

'Are you going to steal my heart now?' I asked him straight out.

Then he gave me the same warm, wise smile as Grandad did, when he'd been about to tell me something nice.

'Your heart beats for both of us, Gregory Peggory. So I don't need to steal it.'

14

Summertime Dangers

Umpin the boggart stood in the bright moonlight, peering deep into my eyes as if he was marvelling that we were still two individuals and not just one.

'We're still standing here, out in the moonlight,' he said at last.

I'd begun to have my doubts about it. I was starting to wonder if we weren't somewhere else, because Umpin seemed to be getting paler and paler, not only his face, but his green boggart's clothes as well.

'The whole thing has probably just been a dream,' I admitted. That was rather sad, I thought, even though the dream had been anything but pleasant. But at this the boggart's cheeks took on more colour.

'My dear young Gregory Peggory,' he began. 'Nothing is *just* a dream. Calling it just a dream is as silly as saying something's just a fact, because a young Peggory prince lives just as much in dreamland as in the other land he comes from.'

I stood looking out over the white, frozen snow that covered the Newt Pond. Beneath the snow and ice the hateful summer lay in wait. As soon as the snow began to melt, the dangers of summertime would reappear.

'Really, all you've done is run away from everything,' Umpin said pensively.

I thought it was unfair of him to lay all the blame on me for running away from the summertime dangers.

'When things get really bad, all you can do is run away,' I said in as grown-up a way as I could.

Umpin shook his small boggart head.

'Anyone who runs away from a bad dream will return to the same dream again and again. A bad dream should be dealt with in exactly the same way you deal with a wolf you meet in the forest.'

'How?' I enquired. I hadn't met many wolves in my life.

'If you meet a wolf, you mustn't take to your heels. The wolf will chase you, and a wolf can run much faster than a Peggory prince. You should stand your ground and stare into the wolf's green eyes and deep inside its head. Then it will be the wolf that'll run off and hide, or turn as gentle as a lamb, and lick your hand. That's the way to deal with the dangers of summertime, too. That's how to deal with queens and lord chamberlains.'

'I don't think so,' I said emphatically. 'That queen is so wicked there's no knowing what she might come up with next time.'

Umpin began to poke at the snow with one foot.

'You can never be sure. She may be good at heart.'

This made me angry. 'How can you think she's good at heart when she threw us into the dungeon?'

'More is possible than a young Peggory prince can know,' was all he said.

He stood a long time looking out over the Newt Pond. Then he went on:

'All along you've allowed yourself to be frightened by the dangers of summer. Now you've got to show you're stronger than they are. If you don't, they'll hound you for the rest of your life. That's why you must return to the great castle.'

I thought Umpin had said some very wise things, as he had so many times before.

But even so I couldn't contemplate rushing back to the castle.

'What if I get lost in the dream?' I said.

Umpin began to pace about on the snow as if he was

suddenly in a hurry for
some reason.

'Something quite
different has been lost
in the dream: it's the
key to something or
other. You can't have
forgotten that you had
a key round your neck
when you were tripping
about here in the half-light
and didn't know in from
out.'

He squinted up at me as if he'd just
divulged a huge secret.

'That newt can't sit behind bars forever, either,'
he went on. 'It would be far too cruel a
punishment, even for a newt.'

When he said newt, and then repeated it, I went
rigid with fear.

'I don't dare go back to summertime's dangers!' I
blurted out.

'I see,' said Umpin flatly, 'but if you don't go and
get that key, you'll never go back to your mum and
dad in that big house with the terrace and deck
chairs either.'

'I can always ring the doorbell,' I said.

'Of course you can, but I don't think it will be your mum or dad who'll answer. More likely it'll be the queen or the lord chamberlain standing in the doorway. For if you lose the key to your own family in a dream castle, the people who live in that dream castle will move into your real house. And those who live in the real house will take up residence in the dream castle. This and much more besides can be found in a very old book.'

I had to swallow a couple of times before Umpin's words sank in, but I had no reason to doubt the truth of them, since the boggart had said so many wise things already.

'So that's settled,' he said finally. 'I'll see you over the boundary into summer straight away. That's a journey Peggory princes can't make without a boggart's help.'

I felt myself quaking under my nightclothes.

'You must take my hand, Gregory Peggory!' said Umpin.

The next instant we were by the Newt Pond again. Once more I was wearing my smart princely clothes, but now it was no longer night. It wasn't broad daylight either, but so early in the morning that night had only just begun to loosen its grip.

A thin curtain of mist hung over the Newt Pond, and above the mist the sky was cranberry-red. The sun would soon rise on a new day. Hosts of frogs were croaking at the water's edge, but they were just ordinary frogs like the ones you can see by the thousand on any normal Sunday.

'I don't think I mentioned that boggarts can never visit the same castle twice, Gregory Peggory,' said Umpin. 'So I wish you the best of luck at the castle. Just have the courage to look all dangers straight in the eye and you'll have nothing to fear.'

These were the very last words Umpin spoke. One of his arms began to disappear, then one of his legs vanished, and so he gradually retreated to the other side of the air.

I was left alone in the dawn light. My bare feet felt cold and I thought how lovely it would be to have a warm duvet to spread over them, because here the entire forest was wide open. I felt sad, too, because I knew I'd never see Umpin the boggart again.

15

The Key

I walked along the path and began my journey back to the castle. After a while I caught sight of one of the big frogs. It came hopping down from the king's garden. I stopped at once and looked it straight in the eye. At that, it turned round and slunk back up to the castle.

Soon I was standing before the castle gate through which, long before, I'd clattered with Umpin and Prince Garamond. Smoke still hung over the castle yard from the remnants of the bonfire.

The royal family were seated round the table on the lawn, even though it was so early in the morning. The lord chamberlain was sitting on his judgement-seat, his arms folded, staring down at them.

No sooner had I entered the castle yard than the queen stood up and pointed at me, and the all others turned.

'Gregory Peggory!' she shouted. 'Come here immediately!'

She obviously thought I wouldn't dare, but I

walked straight towards her, while I practised looking straight into her eyes. I made a polite bow because I hadn't forgotten she was a real queen, but then I stared up at her without wavering, even though she was still wearing nothing on top.

Now it was her turn to look down at the ground, not mine.

'Please go and fetch me a T-shirt, Aurora,' she said.

The princess soon returned with a mauve T-shirt which the queen pulled over her head.

'How are you all, ladies and gentlemen?' I asked, imitating Dad when he was being very polite.

'We've been extremely happy ever since you and that boggart, Umpin, were thrown into the dungeon,' said the lord chamberlain.

I could see that was true, because the family were playing cards, which was my favourite pastime. But I didn't flinch on that account.

'We're playing King of Hearts,' the queen explained.

She said it in a very sweet and pleasant tone. She probably didn't dare to be cross any more after I'd looked her in the eye.

'The person who's left holding the King of Hearts has won the game,' she went on. 'And you can't trump with eights or anything else.'

'Is that why that trumped-up lord chamberlain isn't playing?' I wanted to know.

The lord chamberlain leaped violently in his judgement-seat at this piece of cheek. It was the king who answered:

'He can't play, my good Peggory prince, because he's able to read everyone's thoughts. As a talent, it's often very useful, but it can easily be abused in card games.'

'Do you want to play?' asked Aurora, making room for me between herself and Prince Garamond.

'Thanks for asking,' I said. 'I'd like to, but I've more important things to do first.' I turned away and began to climb the stairs that led into the castle.

'But Gregory Peggory,' said the kind king, 'won't you first tell us what's so important?'

I faced them all and said:

'When I was here last, so many things happened all at once that, unfortunately, I forgot something in the castle's high turret, and it's the key to some thing or other.'

'Is that so?' asked the kind king.

Then he turned and said to the queen:

'I really think this lad has found the key to the whole mystery.'

I didn't know what he meant by that, but I noticed that the lord chamberlain became uneasy. The queen's nose twitched a little, too.

'Is he to be allowed to go up to the tower all by himself?' she asked, as if she was worried I might fall and get hurt myself.

The lord chamberlain coughed twice.

'I don't think he should,' he said. 'In the first place, you can never tell what these Peggory princes might get up to if given the run of a noble castle. And secondly, he was the one who got the queen to put on a T-shirt. That's something he learnt from Umpin the boggart. All boggarts know how to control other people's thoughts.'

'Rubbish!' retorted the queen. 'I put on my T-shirt because I was feeling cold. Besides, I don't care for the way you poke your nose into things that don't concern you.'

She lowered her gaze from the pompous lord chamberlain and looked down at me.

'Come down as soon as you've finished, then, Gregory,' she said. 'There's something I must talk to you about.'

I thought it a bit odd that she was suddenly calling me Gregory.

When I'd got half way up the castle steps, I

turned and looked out over the king's garden. I could see all the giant frogs from South America between the trees and deck-chairs, and now I noticed that one or two at least had bells round their necks. I could hear the tinkling of the bells all the way up the steps.

I had seen cows and sheep with bells near where Flora lived. I even think I saw a horse wearing a bell once. But it was the very first time I'd seen a frog with one.

Once inside the castle, I quickly made my way up all the stairs and rushed up to the room at the top of the tower. As I got near, I heard some dreadful snorting noises.

It was obvious I'd arrived in the nick of time.

The newt had grown so much since last I'd seen him that he'd begun to bulge out between the bars of the cage.

'Let . . . me . . . out!' he gasped as soon as he caught sight of me.

I stooped and retrieved the key from the floor.

'You'll soon be out of that cage,' I said, 'but first you must tell me what you and the other newts at the castle were planning.'

The newt looked up at me with eyes like black gooseberries. They were so piercing that they bored into my face, but I stared back into the black dots without letting my gaze waver.

'I . . . caan't . . . doo . . . zaat,' he said. It was as if the words were tiny newts crawling out of his mouth.

'I promeezed . . . not too geeve . . . zees . . . seecret . . . plaan . . . awaay . . . to Peggoree preences . . . or . . . Umpeen poggarts.'

At first I'd thought he wasn't very good at talking, but now it struck me that perhaps he might be speaking with a French accent.

'Very interesting,' I said. 'But if you won't tell me the truth, you won't get let out either, and you'll just have to stay in there for ever and ever.'

Just then he gave a twist and the whole of his fat tail suddenly popped out from between the bars.

'Zen . . . I . . . tell . . . yoou . . . anyway,' he groaned.

'Why did you steal the king's heart?' I asked.

He pressed his nose right up to the bars of the cage, peered up at me with his gooseberry eyes and said:

'Wee were . . . to . . . taake powerr . . . een zee castle . . . and buurn . . . zee keeng . . . and ees . . . familee . . . on zee bonfire.'

'Did the queen make all the plans?' I wanted to know.

'No,' he whispered feebly. 'Shee eez compleetely . . . innocent.'

Only now did I realise that the newt was talking so strangely because he could barely breathe in the narrow cage.

'Pleaaze . . . let mee ouut,' he implored.

I put the key into the padlock, but first asked:

'Who was it who decided you were to take power in the castle?'

'It . . . waas . . . zee . . . lord chamberlain!'

At that I turned the key, and the fat newt tumbled out of the cage. He lay on the floor wobbling like a great green jelly.

'Now you're free,' I said. 'But you've taken part in a terrible plot. Promise you'll never do anything like that again.'

The whole of his podgy body rippled several times in consent.

'Now we must hurry down to the king's garden and arrest the lord chamberlain at once,' I said.

I opened the door and pushed the newt before me. He began to roll down the stairs, but quickly got up on two legs and ran as fast as he was able. When we got out of the castle we tore down the steps so fast I was afraid he might be shaken to pieces before we'd managed to capture the lord chamberlain.

16

The Lord Chamberlain

I chased the newt into the king's garden. There was still a little morning mist between the trees and shrubs, but the sky was a mass of small red puffy clouds chased by the sun, which still had not risen.

As we approached the others, I realised that they were playing leapfrog. The lord chamberlain was being the frog, and all the others were leaping over him.

'This frog has done a lot of lying, I'm afraid,' I shouted at the top of my voice. 'So you can never trust him!'

They stopped playing immediately. The lord chamberlain straightened himself up and brushed down his smart uniform, trying at the same time to stare into my eyes.

'What sort of nonsense is this?' demanded the queen.

'This lord chamberlain isn't quite as innocent as you think,' I said. 'He plotted to burn you all on the bonfire.'

Just then they caught sight of the newt.

'What's this I see?' exclaimed the queen. 'I thought all the newts were in their dungeon long ago.'

The lord chamberlain wasn't quite so starchy now. He'd brushed all the grass off, but it still looked as if he itched all over.

'There was one newt left,' I said. 'I'd locked him up in the tower. And a good thing too, since I was able to hear the truth about the queen and the lord chamberlain.'

They began to take their places at the table. The lord chamberlain looked about as if wondering whether flight might be the best plan, but that would be as good as admitting to all the bad things he'd done, so he sat down at the table as well.

'Listen here, Gregory Peggory,' said the king in

a kindly tone. 'If only the half of what you say is true, and if that's the half about the lord chamberlain wanting to burn us all on the bonfire, it's a most serious matter. The question is simply: how do we know it's true?'

'Quite correct, Your most esteemed Majesty,' said the lord chamberlain with a haughty smile. 'This Peggory prince isn't a true prince. He's nothing but a lowly forest prince who's sneaked into the castle in the company of a boggart. Even his tales aren't true.'

'He's lying!' I shouted. 'It's him who isn't a proper lord chamberlain. He was the wicked boggart who turned Prince Garamond into a thousand tadpoles.'

At this the lord chamberlain laughed so uproariously that for a while it sounded as if he would drown in his own laughter.

The queen found a clever way of settling the dispute.

'This discussion is both silly and unnecessary,' she said, 'while there's someone amongst us who can read everyone's thoughts. Lord Chamberlain, I command that you mount your judgement-seat right away!'

The lord chamberlain obeyed the queen's order at once, and for a moment I was

worried that I'd been foolish again, because
I remembered what had happened the last time
he had sat in his judgement-seat. Perhaps the
most sensible thing might be to run away. But
Umpin had said I couldn't leave the castle's
dangers like that. So instead, I quickly began
staring into the lord chamberlain's eyes. And
just to make sure, I pulled a face at him as
well.

'Lord Chamberlain,' the queen began, 'would
you be so kind as to tell us if it's true that you

helped build the big midsummer bonfire to roast your own king and queen on, or if this is just some fanciful fairy tale?'

The lord chamberlain had folded his arms. It was obvious that he felt secure all the time he sat in his judgement-seat and took orders from the queen.

'This tale is a tissue of lies, Your Majesty,' he said. 'Therefore I sentence this Peggory prince to be drowned in the Dark Cauldron before the clock strikes eleven.'

'Oh no!' shouted Princess Aurora, and hurled her yo-yo straight at the lord chamberlain's face. Prince Garamond, too, sprang to his feet and banged the table with his sharp sword.

'Silence!' commanded the queen. 'We have heard the lord chamberlain's clear evidence.'

At this the king cleared his throat three times, but the queen continued to address the lord chamberlain.

'Would you also be so kind as to read your own thoughts?'

The lord chamberlain nearly fell off his seat in sheer terror.

'*Read your own thoughts!*' repeated the queen in a stern voice.

'Well, I was thinking that . . . ' the lord

chamberlain began, but stopped because he got a
fit of coughing.

'*What* were you thinking?' the queen asked again.
'You must answer immediately. If you hesitate I'll
know you're telling lies.'

She looked him hard in the eyes.

'I was thinking . . . that it's true that I cast a spell
over all the newts in the castle to take the entire
royal family prisoner and burn you all on the
bonfire so I could assume power here and be king

myself. I was also thinking that it's true what this Peggory prince said: that it was I who bewitched the prince and turned him into all those stupid tadpoles.'

With that he collapsed in his high chair.

'So, this Peggory prince was right,' said the king. 'And he's saved us all from a terrible tragedy.'

No one said anything straight away, but then the king spoke again.

'Even now the *full* story hasn't come out. Gregory Peggory said that the newt told him the truth about the lord chamberlain *and* the queen. May we hear the truth about the queen too?'

The king looked up at the lord chamberlain in his high chair after casting an anxious glance at his beloved queen.

'The truth is that she's a cunning witch who's wicked and nasty into the bargain,' he said.

When the queen heard this accusation she just started laughing, and I did too, but I only laughed to myself. I laughed to myself so much that my spine started tingling, because I knew that what the lord chamberlain had said about the queen wasn't true.

'And now, perhaps, you'd be kind enough to read the thoughts you were *thinking* while you stated that I was a cunning witch,' the queen said.

'Hm . . . I was thinking that the queen is completely innocent,' said the lord chamberlain and slumped down again.

'Has the whole truth been told now?' the king enquired again. 'You needn't answer that. You might as well read your own thoughts straight away, it will save us loads of time.'

The lord chamberlain coughed and spluttered.

'I was thinking that only half the truth has come out,' he said. 'The other half is that the queen was being rather difficult yesterday, but that was only because I'd stared right into her head to make her wicked and nasty to Gregory Peggory and Umpin the boggart, though neither had done anything wrong. I also cast a spell on her to make her let out all the water from the wells in the king's garden, so that they would drown in the Dark Cauldron.'

This was a huge surprise to everyone sitting at the table.

'That's quite the meanest thing I've heard in a long while!' the queen exclaimed. 'But now that horrid spell is broken!'

She shook her shoulders and rubbed her eyes.
Then she put her arm round me and gave me a
lovely hug.

'It's never nice being angry with people you like,'
she said.

I had to hold my breath to prevent myself from
crying, because the queen had given me a hug.
Deep down I'd wanted to be her friend ever since
I first came to the castle.

'So it was the lord chamberlain who was the spy here in the castle,' said Prince Garamond suddenly. 'I see it isn't only in card games that you can cheat if you can read other people's thoughts. You can even cheat the king out of his heart and half his kingdom. The lord chamberlain must be severely punished for this.'

The queen rose again and looked up at the lord chamberlain.

'You heard what he said. Now we want to have judgement.'

I almost felt sorry for the wicked lord chamberlain. Having sentence passed on you can be bad enough, without having to do it yourself.

'I am sentenced to flee from the king's garden and all the lovely forests surrounding it,' he said mournfully. 'I am further sentenced never to return.'

The queen looked at her husband.

'Can we accept that judgement, my lord?'

The king nodded. 'But it must be put into effect at once,' he added.

The prince rose and struck the table twice with his sword.

The lord chamberlain climbed down from his high chair and stood looking at us.

'You can leave that smart uniform on the table,'

said the queen. 'It belongs to the castle.'

Without hesitating, the lord chamberlain undressed, and stood cowering in nothing but his underwear.

'And now, the quicker you get out of here the better,' said the king.

The lord chamberlain glanced over at the newt who'd been waiting silently in the bushes watching the proceedings. No one had given him a thought.

'Take them all prisoner and throw them in the dungeon!' the lord chamberlain shouted.

The fat newt came charging towards us, but I stared him in the eyes so he ground to a halt at the last moment.

'You're not to capture us,' was all I said. 'Instead, you can help us by chasing the lord chamberlain out of this forest.'

I didn't need to say more, because the newt began chasing the lord chamberlain, while the lord chamberlain tried to run even faster. Both were shouting and yelling. They rushed down towards the Newt Pond, never to return.

17

Sunrise

After the lord chamberlain had fled from the newt, and the curse of the entire castle, as fast as his legs could carry him, we sat nice and peacefully round the table. Soon the queen got up and said that she had to make a little speech about all the odd goings on at the castle.

'Dear, good Peggory prince,' she began. 'This is the start of a splendid day. At last I've been freed from the spell that was making me so wicked and nasty to you and Umpin the boggart. How I could have been so blind to the temptations of wickedness remains a riddle, a riddle we won't try to guess at now, because now everything is as it was before I was bewitched. The truth is that I like young Peggory princes more than anything else. From now on you'll always be welcome at the castle.'

The prince and princess stood up and clapped.

'Hooray!' shouted Aurora in delight, and came round the table and took my hands. 'Now we can make garlands of flowers!'

It was strange she was talking about garlands. Flora and I used to make them. We'd fill up a whole basket, and then stand at the garden gate and sell them to any passers-by who wanted to brighten up their dull, grey day. And that would make our day brighter too, because we'd get money for ice-creams and chocolate.

'Gregory Peggory has been so brave that he'll be more than just welcome at the castle,' said the king. 'I command that this Peggory prince be made a Knight of the Order of the Garden Table. In addition, he shall receive a lovely diploma because he was able to avoid all the dangers of the castle like a true diplomat. Not only has he managed to control his own thoughts, but he's managed to control the wicked lord chamberlain's thoughts too, so that the whole truth came out.'

Then he beckoned to his two children and went on: 'You can do the diploma, Princess Aurora. And

Prince Garamond can dub Gregory Peggory a knight.'

The princess ran into the castle, while Prince Garamond advanced towards me and told me to kneel on the ground before him. Then he slapped me hard on the shoulder with his sword. It hurt a bit, but now that I was a real knight I had to be able to put up with that sort of thing. The king and queen clapped.

Just then, Aurora came running down the castle steps with a diploma in one hand and an ice-cream in the other.

Prince Gregory Peggory

*has on this splendid day
been made knight of the
garden table
because he fought the wicked
lord chamberlain
and the slimy newts.
for this he is also to become
this castle's diplomat.
may his fine heart
always beat
for everything
good!*

While I licked the ice-cream, the king read out what was on the diploma, written in the finest hand a princess can manage:

When the king finished reading, I thought again of what had happened while Mum was at the castle in France. All the nice things that had happened here wouldn't bring my grandad back to life.

I wasn't able to dwell on it for long, as the kind king now said that he wanted to show me the sunrise from a little hill behind the castle. He said he would also tell me a secret when we were up there. He took me by the hand, commanding the others to go inside the castle and clear up after the festivities.

We strolled along a narrow path amongst the shrubs and trees of the king's garden. I always used to go for long walks with Grandad and as we went, it seemed to me that the king became more and more like Grandad.

Gradually, as we neared the summit, the Newt Pond and the white castle got smaller and smaller. At the same time I realised that the forest was larger than I'd imagined.

'You're very sad about your grandad, aren't you?' said the king as we walked along.

I looked down at the moss and heather and

nodded my head.

'Was that why you made sure I
got my heart back after the newts had
stolen it?' he asked.

It struck me as an odd question. It had never
crossed my mind.

I shook my head and looked up at him. Now he
seemed so like my grandad that I was just waiting
for him to pull out a pipe and start smoking it, like

Grandad used to do when we got to a hilltop or were sitting in the boat waiting for the fish to bite.

When we'd got to the top of the hill, we turned and gazed out over the forest. Down below, the castle looked just like some tiny fairy castle, the same size as Flora's dolls' house down south. Behind the castle we could see the Newt Pond, and from here it looked no bigger than a puddle.

I could tell it would be a fine day. The sun was about to rise in the east, and the small red puffs of cloud raced faster and faster across the sky. Far below I could see the frogs with bells grazing amongst the shrubs and trees of the king's garden. Away in the distance we caught sight of a lone newt chasing the treacherous lord chamberlain.

'They must have decided to run to the ends of the earth,' I said, pointing down at them.

The king nodded solemnly.

'When lord chamberlains and newts like that get going, you can never stop them.'

He said this in a voice so like Grandad's that I looked up at him in surprise.

And then – I saw that this king *was* my grandad, and he was wearing exactly the same wise smile.

'Grandad!' I yelled, and wrapped my arms around him.

In that instant he seemed almost disappointed that I'd found out his secret before he'd been able to tell it, but soon he was ruffling my hair.

'Sit down here, lad,' he said simply and motioned to a large boulder which we both went and sat down on.

He said nothing to begin with, but stared deep into my eyes. Perhaps he was looking right into my head where all my thoughts were.

'Gregory Peggory,' he said. 'Even though I've begun to look more and more like your grandad, and even though one day I'll be so like him that no one will be able to tell the difference, he'll never be able to return to the house with the terrace and the deck chairs. But, then, he doesn't need to. Because now your grandad has made his home in your heart.'

I felt very disappointed by what he'd told me. I pouted a bit.

'A whole grandad can't fit into a small boy's heart,' I said.

He began to stroke my hair while I stared and stared at all the red clouds that raced up above us, faster than a bird can fly.

'Where there's love for a big grandad,' he said as he went on stroking my head, 'there'll be room for him as well. But this is only half of the truth. The other half is that your grandad has also made his home in your eyes.'

'Pooh!' I said as I shook my head slightly to make him stop stroking. 'If Grandad's gone, he can't possibly see what's going on.'

'But weren't you your grandad's very best friend?' said the king.

I nodded.

'Do you think he would believe what you said you saw – even if he hadn't seen it himself?'

I nodded again, because now I remembered a time I'd seen a rabbit outside Grandma and Grandad's house. When I'd rushed in and told Grandad, he just said he didn't need to get up from the sofa and look at what I'd seen, because I'd already seen it. And there were lots of other times too when he'd asked me to look at things for him . . . One evening Grandad asked me to look at the moon, because he was so tired he just wanted to sleep, but he still wanted to know if there was a full moon.

'Can you see the forest down there?' the king went on. 'Can you see the world stretching as far as your eye can reach?'

Again, I could only nod.

'Then I believe that will do for your grandad,

too. So both of us can sit here and watch the sunrise together.'

As he said the word 'sunrise', the bright sun rose from behind the mountains in the east, and at precisely that moment the king vanished. He retreated to that land which is on the other side of the air, just like Umpin the boggart. I didn't find it all that strange, because the sun was rising on a new day.

No sooner had the king, or my grandad, gone, than I saw a flock of sparrows descend from the sky. Thirty or forty birds chirruped at one another as if they were all laughing, and then I had to laugh too. I laughed and laughed, as if the whole day had been created just for laughter.

I sat on, looking out over the wide forest. I watched the birds which flew so easily, so lightly, over all the trees of the forest. Snakes and newts no longer rustled in the grass, and boggarts and fairy-tale kings had returned to that place from which such beings come.

Now the night had passed, and the sun began to tinge the castle's white towers with yellow. All around me lay the great, thick forest as the sun climbed higher and higher into the sky.

If you have enjoyed reading
The Frog Castle,
you will like these other books
by Jostein Gaarder.

Hello? Is Anybody There?

Translated by James Anderson
Illustrated by Sally Gardner

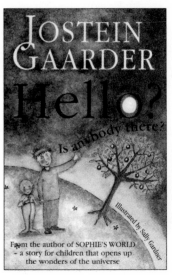

Hens, dinosaurs, astronauts and
a white rabbit all have a part to play
in this magical, mind-blowing story
of Joe's encounter with a little alien
who tumbles out of a spaceship into
his garden.

'Gaarder's major achievement . . . is
to alert children to the potential of
their own thinking, and to extend a
natural sense of awe . . . There are
echoes of Saint-Exupery's *The Little
Prince* . . . in the gentle tone of this
mind-stretching tale.'
School Librarian

The Christmas Mystery

Translated by Elizabeth Rokkan
Colour pictures by Rosemary Wells

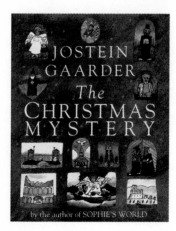

The windows in an old
Advent calendar open to reveal
to a present-day boy the story
of a girl who disappeared years
ago and travelled back in time
to Bethlehem to witness the birth
of Christ.

'a skilful and lasting achievement,
with all the elements of a perfect
Christmas tale'
The Times